SAM FRIEDMAN

Spikes

The Story of the First Lady of Baseball, as told to Jackie Robinson

First published by Sam's View From The Press Box Publishing 2024

This novel is entirely a work of fiction. The names, characters and incidents portrayed in it are the work of the author's imagination. Any resemblance to actual persons, living or dead, events or localities is entirely coincidental.

Cover image courtesy of freepik (www.freepik.com)

First edition

ISBN: 979-8-9912344-0-5

This book was professionally typeset on Reedsy. Find out more at reedsy.com

This story is dedicated to:

My darling wife, Cheryl, for her unbounded love and support, and for always believing in me

Mel Glenn, for his keen editing eye and for including me in his writing class for retired teachers, which inspired me to revisit and reimagine "Spikes"

Jackie Robinson, who courageously broke barriers and paved the way for others to follow him

For women athletes, who are capable of doing anything if given a fair chance to compete

Contents

Chapter 1: Noon

Dear Jackie,

I get why the title of your autobiography was, "I Never Had It Made," because neither did I. Yet here I am, about to make my Major League debut on April 15, 2029, 82 years to the day since you broke baseball's color barrier. This should be the happiest moment of my life, but all I can think about is what if I fail, and in front of all these people? It's seven hours until game time, but I can't sit still, so I'm pacing back and forth in my personal locker room, graciously vacated by two ballgirls. I'm dictating this message to you partly to pass the time as I'm all alone, unable to dress and shower with my teammates. But even if I had someone around to talk to, no other person on Earth except you could possibly appreciate what I'm going through or the gravity of what I'm about to do.

Only you, Jackie, could know what it's like to feel the weight of the world on your shoulders while dressing for a baseball game. To be judged and found unworthy by millions before you've played a single inning. To be among teammates who don't know what to make of you—whether to feel proud or embarrassed, thrilled or furious, supportive or determined to see you fail.

I'd like to think you would have my back if we played together, the way Pee Wee Reese shrugged off his racist upbringing in Kentucky to literally embrace you, ignoring death threats to drape his arm about your shoulders on the field in front of a bloodthirsty Cincinnati crowd. I'd hate to think you would have displayed the same blind, ignorant prejudice against me because of what I am as you had to overcome just for being different. I choose to think you'd be better than that and would at least support me on principle—although I suppose I couldn't blame you if you had your doubts about playing second base behind someone like me on the mound.

You changed the game and the world when you jogged out of the dugout to play first base at Ebbets Field for the Brooklyn Dodgers 62 years before I was born, yet I feel as if I've known you all my life. I've read every book written about you, studied newsreel footage, memorized interviews, and worn out the DVD of "42," the movie where Chad Boseman brought you back to life in all your glory and agony. I wish you were here to talk me through today's trial, or at least witness what I'm about to do, but you passed in 1972—way too young at 53. Will the pressure I'm under to prove everyone wrong about my right to be here shorten my life as well?

It may sound crazy, but it's always given me comfort talking to you over the years, even if it's only in my imagination. It gives me strength to feel your presence as I follow in your footsteps and try to follow the example you set.

In case you don't remember me, I'm Kristine Randall, although everyone has called me "Spikes" at the ballpark since I was eight. A dozen years later, I'm still way too slight to convince most people I'm a professional athlete let alone intimidate opponents, standing on tiptoes at five feet, seven inches while barely clearing 150 pounds in full uniform. I absolutely refused to use any of the pink baseball gloves well-meaning relatives gave me over the years, but I've always kept my dirty blonde ponytail flopping above the strap keeping my cap on tight. A few weeks short of turning 21, I'm not yet old enough to drink champagne legally if things turn out well today, or do shots of something a lot harder if I get clobbered.

It helps a little to be pitching for the New York Mets, whose former owner was a Brooklyn Dodger fanatic who worshiped you, Jackie. I played my first minor league season for the Brooklyn Cyclones, the Mets' High-A farm team at Maimonides Park, where a statue of you with Pee Wee welcomes fans at the front gate. When my promotion to the majors was announced here at Citi Field, I was introduced to the media in the Jackie Robinson Rotunda, where a huge banner greeting fans as they ride up the escalator quotes you as saying: "A life is not important except for the impact it has on other lives."

Only now do I fully understand what you meant, as hundreds of young girls waited for hours outside the stadium to greet me when I arrived for my historic debut, their eyes wide and smiles even wider as I autographed gloves, hats, shirts, and baseball cards. They squealed after I posed with them for selfies. They told me how I had inspired them to keep playing baseball in Little League, high school, and college, vowing to one day join me in the big leagues. One reporter said that not since Caitlin Clark sent TV ratings through the roof for women shooting hoops in college and the WNBA, back in 2024, has anyone drawn so much attention for being a ball-playing girl!

I'm proud of all I did to get here, but what if I'm not good enough today? What if I fall on my face and get sent back down to the minors? What if I get released one day without ever having another shot up here? Will Major League Baseball ever let a woman play again? How could I let down millions of girls counting on me to prove everyone wrong about women being no match for men in sports?

Sorry, Jackie, but the team publicist says it's time for my photo shoot... Catch you later!

Chapter 2: 1 p.m.

Dear Jackie,

As a pitcher I have it easier than you did in some ways, but in others it's much harder for me. While you had to take the field and face abuse every game, I'll only pitch once or twice a week if I'm a starter, or for an inning or two if I stay in the bullpen as a reliever. But unlike you, I'll be the center of attention every time I take the mound. I can't blend into the infield, forgotten until a ball is hit or thrown my way, in the spotlight only when I step up to hit three or four times per game. The ball is always in my hands, which means I must prove myself with every pitch.

It would help if I could throw almost 100 miles-per-hour like most everybody else here. No one would dare mock me then, knowing I could stick tormentors in the ribs or knock them on their ass with some chin music. But unfortunately, the speed gun barely registers my velocity, topping out at about 65 mph— slower than most batting practice pitches for major leaguers. I hit that peak at 13 as the ace of my Jackie Robinson Little League team, pitching the Brooklyn Eagles all the way to Williamsport, Pa. I hoisted the championship trophy after blowing my fastball by the final batter to win baseball's only true World Series, striking out 18 and shutting out a very talented squad from Taiwan.

Life was so much simpler back then, Jackie. I was just one of the boys, which is all I've ever wanted to be. Oh, sure, there were disgruntled parents grumbling about a girl taking their son's roster spot. And every team had at least one insecure jerk who thought he could bully me. But besides bloodying a few noses along the way, I let my pitching speak for itself. If you can't get batters out, you can't play. But if you're able to mow down hitters, they keep handing you the ball no matter what type of equipment you carry beneath your uniform.

After Little League it was biology that finally got the best of me, not sexism. While testosterone started boosting the height, weight, strength, and velocity for the boys on my team, I was left undersized and virtually defenseless on the mound. My fastball was no longer overpowering, and my curve broke too slightly to fool anyone. I lifted weights and took whatever legal supplements I could get my hands on, but it wasn't enough for me to keep up, so I got my clock cleaned trying out for the Lincoln High baseball squad. Lincoln's coach, Mel Glenn, who managed me in Little League, was kind and encouraging, urging me to try out for the girls' softball team. But after a few lame attempts at throwing underhand, I knew my heart wasn't in it. I just couldn't stomach giving up hardball, where the best of the best play the game I loved.

My dream could've ended right there, but luckily my dad is as big a baseball fanatic as I am. Harold Randall loved watching me play and took it just as hard when it looked as if I'd reached the end of the line. A few days after my failed tryout he suggested we make our long overdue pilgrimage to baseball's Mecca in Cooperstown, a sleepy village in Upstate New York where Abner Doubleday supposedly invented the game and where the greatest of all time are ensconced in the Hall of Fame. I tried to beg off— it was too painful to even think about baseball just then—but Dad insisted. I moped most of the way up, drowning out his chipper chatter with noise-canceling headphones.

However, my whole attitude changed once we entered the hallowed Hall showcasing the game's immortals. It was a religious experience. The structure itself took my breath away, magnificent in its simplicity and elegance. It was as quiet as a cathedral, with visitors speaking in hushed tones, as befitting the Church of Baseball. The ceiling was very high, but the bronze plaques adorning the wood-paneled walls were conveniently mounted at eye level for the average-sized fan. We didn't have time to closely examine hundreds of plaques but of course I lingered by yours, Jackie—touching it gently, reverently— lovingly tracing my index finger along the outline of your portrait. I choked back tears, so sorry to have disappointed you, my dad, and myself.

Lightheaded and exhausted after spending the morning at baseball's Mount Olympus, I didn't feel like touring the rest of the museum. But Dad took my arm and nearly dragged me upstairs to check out an exhibit he said I absolutely had to see before we left, leading me straight to "Diamond Dreams: Women in Baseball." The first display to catch my eye was the uniform of Mo'ne Davis, who in 2014 became the first girl to

7

earn a win and pitch a shutout in the Little League World Series. After watching her masterpiece on TV with Dad when I was just six years old, I begged him to buy me a ball and glove, putting aside my dolls and vowing to become a star pitcher in my own right.

I also paid my respects to the handful of women heralded for playing professionally in non-affiliated independent leagues, such as Illa Borders in the late 1990s and Kelsie Whitmore in the 2020s. I lingered by the uniforms of the Colorado Silver Bullets, a team of pioneering women barnstorming the country in the mid-1990s playing hardball against men in college and semi-pro leagues. I saluted Toni Stone, who played second base for two seasons as the Negro Leagues wound down in the 1950s. And I tipped my cap to pictures of players from the All-American Girls Professional Baseball League, which lasted for a decade after its mid-1940s launch—made famous in my favorite movie, 1992's "A League of Their Own." Too bad no one would ever see me featured in this exhibit, I thought.

But then Dad steered me to one particular artifact that changed my life—the jersey of Chelsea Baker, donated to the Hall after she tossed two perfect games as a 12-year-old Little Leaguer in 2010, accompanied by a video of her making major leaguers look foolish as a high school pitcher throwing batting practice to the Tampa Bay Rays in 2014. Dad put his arm around my shoulders and pointed to the text below her jersey. It said that Chelsea had been crowned "The Knuckleball Princess," with a picture of the odd way she gripped the ball with the tips of her index and middle fingers.

"Do you think you could throw like that?" Dad whispered. "Phil Niekro, who managed the Silver Bullets, was the greatest knuckleballer who ever lived. If he could make the Hall of Fame throwing that pitch, why couldn't you?"

Why not? After all, I had nothing to lose.

On the drive home I devoured a book illustrating the grips of famous knuckleball pitchers like Hall of Famer Hoyt Wilhelm and "Ball Four" author Jim Bouton, along with Phil Niekro and his brother, Joe. They all emphasized that you don't have to throw hard for a knuckler to be effective, as the handful of those who were able to compete in the majors with this trick pitch rarely broke 70 mph—right in my wheelhouse! We had brought our gloves and a ball to play catch on Doubleday Field, site of the annual Hall of Fame game, so I practiced the grip in the car and even tried to toss a few knucklers to Dad at each rest stop. Its flight was erratic, but the ball definitely moved funny. I could only imagine how crazy it must look darting through the air at a mesmerized batter!

As soon as we got home, Dad, a longtime insurance agent, used his industry connections to get in touch with R.A. Dickey, a Cy Young Award winner with the Mets after resurrecting his career with the knuckler, who had appeared at one of my father's conventions as a motivational speaker. Dickey recommended a local coach here in New York, David M. Katz, a former journeyman pitcher who never made the majors but knew enough to teach a master class in knuckleball techniques.

I also made a stop in Vero Beach, Florida, to work with Mo'ne

Davis herself, who I met after a panel discussion Dad and I attended in Lower Manhattan at your museum, Jackie, on "Leveling the Playing Field" for women in baseball. Mo'ne invited me down to Florida to show her what I had as she coached a whole gaggle of girls with dreams just like mine during Major League Baseball's annual Trailblazer Series—a tournament held at the former "Dodgertown" training complex renamed for you, Jackie! Mo'ne and the rest of the coaching staff were very impressed with my command of the knuckler, which none of the girls playing there could hit.

After putting in a year of hard work perfecting my secret weapon, I showed up for Lincoln High's tryouts once again as a sophomore. Coach Glenn eyed me skeptically as I strode to the mound with the same swagger I displayed as a Little Leaguer, armed with a pitch I knew few if any major leaguers, let alone high school batters, had ever faced. Macho freshman trying out for the team rushed to the head of the line behind the batting cage, eager to dig in against this silly girl, figuring I'd be easy to hit and therefore impress the coaching staff with their prowess.

They had no idea what they were in for.

One after another swung in futility against my knuckler, which danced about like a mischievous butterfly. Now you see it, now you don't! They cocked their bats and lashed out at the elusive ball, only to miss by a foot or more time and time again. Before long, Coach Glenn shooed away the wannabes and ordered his varsity hitters into the lioness' den, but they were dead meat as well. Then Coach Glenn, a slugging first baseman for Lincoln back in the day, stepped in to see for himself why no one could get good wood on my pitches. He was more patient and focused, yet only managed to hit a few weak grounders and popups, fouling off most of my beauties.

"Not too shabby, is she, Mel?" shouted Dad, beaming from the aluminum stands behind home plate. Coach Glenn grinned at his former Lincoln classmate, nodding as put his arm around me on our way to the dugout. "We may have to find a spot for your girl this year, Harry," he said, grinning beneath his shaggy mustache.

I struggled but didn't embarrass myself that first season, winning eight and losing six with an earned run average around four. My control wasn't consistent as I was still learning to master the knuckler. I walked way too many batters and threw more than my share of wild pitches, although it didn't help that my catcher was a sieve, giving up multiple passed balls each game. But I kept working between starts with Dad and Mr. Katz, and by my junior year was dominating hitters like I had in Little League, only with finesse rather than power. In my last two seasons I was 22-6 with a 1.64 ERA, striking out three times as many as I walked, and only allowing a handful of extra base hits.

Yet while lots of colleges scouted me, few recruited me, and none from the big baseball schools in Arizona, California, Florida, Oklahoma, or Texas. And those who did express interest only offered minimal scholarships—usually for softball. A macho high school stud with my stats would've been overwhelmed with offers, or maybe even encouraged to enter the Major League Amateur Draft and go pro. No one would admit they didn't trust a girl to join their team. Those who gave Dad and me any feedback at all either said I was too small or that the knuckler was too risky a pitch. That left me back where I started after Little League— out in the cold, with nowhere to play.

Excuse me, Jackie! That's the trainer with my lunch. I'll get right back to you.

Chapter 3: 2 p.m.

Dear Jackie,

So, there I was, almost ready to give up on baseball yet again, when my dad and Coach Glenn called a Mets scout, Buddy Lawrence, who had seen many of my high school games. Buddy was a former college pitcher—playing hardball as the only woman on the Stanford men's squad. But her dreams of a pro career came to an abrupt end at graduation. After earning a degree in sports management and psychology, Buddy worked with kids, adults, and even some pro players on the mental aspect of baseball, helping those mired in slumps or suffering from a case of the yips keeping them from throwing accurately. She also moonlighted as a bird dog on nights and weekends, checking out local high school and college talent.

Buddy got to know me when I was a Mets ballgirl, a choice gig set up by Coach Glenn through his connections with the scouting staff. It was really cool hanging around the team at Citi Field, even though the work was anything but glamorous. Basically, we were gofers, doing a lot of grunge work—such as cleaning and polishing cleats, cycling through loads of dirty laundry, and rubbing up hundreds of baseballs before each game with "magic mud" from the Delaware River basin so they wouldn't be slippery in the players' hands. But it was all worth it because I got to sit on the field in front of the box seats and watch games while chasing down foul balls.

Even better was getting to pitch batting practice when the coaches' arms were sore or if they were just too tired, especially before day games after night games. Once the coaches heard I pitched for my high school team and saw me throw to a fellow "clubbie" (as we "clubhouse attendants" were formally known), they were happy to delegate BP to me a few times during each homestand. The players loved hammering away at my 70 miles-per-hour fastballs—the very definition of "batting practice pitches"—and appreciated how I could put the ball wherever they wanted it. The only downside was not being able to test my best pitch against them, since the hitters would cuss at me if I tried to sneak a nasty knuckler into the mix.

Buddy was sympathetic to my plight, convinced my knuckleball had Major League potential, yet she also doubted any team would pick me in the amateur draft despite my high school achievements. She said my best bet would be to accept whatever scholarship I could get from any college that would take a chance on me, hoping I'd draw higher-level attention if I continued developing. At least that way I would get an education and have other career options, as she had after Stanford. But she also promised to speak with her superiors in the Mets' front office and see if they might suggest a better alternative, or at least provide a recommendation to help convince a major college to give me a shot.

Imagine my shock, Jackie, when Buddy convinced the team to give me a public tryout after sharing my stats and highlights of my best outings. She confided that while her scouting colleagues were not on board, Met coaches thought the team owed a favor to one of its own after all the hard work I'd put in for them. The clincher was enthusiastic support from the people in marketing and public relations, who saw me as a potential gold mine— likely to generate ticket and souvenir sales as well as goodwill.

A week later, Buddy ushered Dad and I into Maimonides Park, right off the Coney Island boardwalk. Brooklyn's Eiffel Tower, the iconic Parachute Jump, loomed large behind me as I warmed up in the rightfield bullpen. A few local sports reporters and a national TV crew accepted the invitation from PR to witness this most unusual tryout, curious to see a girl auditioning for a cadre of Major League executives—including the head of the Mets' scouting staff, the assistant general manager, and their Major League pitching coach. Buddy stood by the mound, offering encouragement as I tossed one wicked knuckleball after another. I felt sorry for the hapless catcher recruited from the Brooklyn Cyclones, who kept stabbing his mitt at my pitches as if warding off a deranged bird, dropping one out of every three.

"Her ball does move like a son of a bitch," I heard the pitching coach say to the Mets' brain trust. "If we can find someone to catch her, she might cause some problems for hitters, at least down here in the minors."

"And she'd be a terrific draw!" added the head of PR. "We'd sell out every time she's scheduled to pitch!"

"Maybe," yawned the assistant GM, checking his watch. "Before we get carried away, let's see how she handles live batters."

My heart pounded as I walked slowly down the first base line and out to the mound. I'd seen dozens of games at this park with Dad over the years, but it was a lot different pitching here against the Mets' best prospects fresh out of high school, college, and the fertile fields of Latin America. A half-dozen muscle-bound Cyclones lined up in front of the home dugout studying my warm-ups, none appearing eager to get in the batter's box. One-by-one they strode warily to the plate, flashing nervous grins or blinking at me in dismay. I'd bet that most had never hit against a knuckler before, let alone faced a girl. I felt nervous but not intimidated even though these were professional ballplayers, because they were still just gawky teenagers like me.

I pitched fearlessly and showed no mercy, dispensing each batter in short order. A few managed to hit a sharp grounder or high fly—but nothing that wouldn't have been routinely handled by my fielders. The rest kept fouling balls off or missing my pitches entirely, often by six inches or more.

My confidence soared and I was feeling unbeatable until I spotted a familiar face pulling on batting gloves as he emerged from the dugout, approaching the batter's box with far more swagger than the raw A-ball kids I had dazzled. The Mets' all-star catcher and former Cyclone great, Francisco Alvarez, rehabbing with Brooklyn after a stint on the injured list, smiled amiably as he stepped up to the plate.

"You don't mind if I take a few swings, do you, Spikes?" he

16

asked, rhetorically, planting his right foot in the dirt without waiting for a response from me or the suits. The reporters by the third base dugout mumbled to one another and paid closer attention, jostling with the TV crew pushing to get in front of them for a clear line of sight.

Even though I had thrown batting practice to Francisco hundreds of times over the past two seasons, I had never tried to sneak one of my patented knucklers past him, warned by the coaches not to upset their slugger's timing. Remember, BP was all about letting players hit, not trying to get them out. This was a whole different ballgame.

Yet this wouldn't be the first time he had seen my "out" pitch in action. While heralded for his home runs, Francisco prided himself on his defense behind the plate and skill in handling a pitching staff. It was he who actually invited me into the bullpen from time to time, determined to learn how to catch a knuckleball just in case such a hurler ever joined his team. He struggled at first, but soon managed to snag most of them. My knuckler would be no mystery to Francisco.

I stepped off the mound to compose myself before digging my toe along the rubber for better leverage. I kept my head down, stalling for time. Whether the Mets had purposely brought Alvarez in as a ringer to see what kind of stuff I really had, or whether Francisco had decided to join the party to satisfy his own curiosity didn't matter. Facing a Major League star would almost certainly decide my fate.

"What's the holdup?" Francisco shouted, his booming voice

17

shattering the silence in the empty stadium like the crack of a bat sending a line drive at me. "Vamanos! Let's go!!!"

I was so nervous my first pitch slipped rather than snapped off my fingertips, flattening rather than fluttering as it crossed the plate. Francisco took a vicious uppercut and rocketed the ball to dead center. I froze on the mound with my back to him, shoulders slumping as I watched his blast clear the fence 420 feet away. But I snapped out of my funk when Francisco started berating me, the way he would while trying to revive his pitchers during games when they faltered and seemed on the verge of being knocked out.

"That can't be the best stuff you've got, amiga! Are you still a ballgirl throwing BP? Or is your damned knuckler not good enough to get me out?"

I turned around and glared at Alvarez, but by then his manufactured rage was gone as quickly as it was generated. Still, I was fuming, determined to wipe that goofy grin off his face. From then on my knuckler broke like crazy. "That's more like it!" he nodded, driving a few hits with authority, but laughing at his own futility as most of his batted balls skidded harmlessly on the ground or popped lazily above the infield, while he lunged at and missed a dozen pitches entirely.

Sweating profusely by the end of our 30-pitch showdown, Francisco tipped his helmet and pointed my way with his bat as he passed the Mets execs. "You better sign her," he said, "if only so I won't have to face her again when she's pitching for some other team. She's not any easier to hit than she is to catch!"

A few days later, after I was predictably ignored in baseball's amateur draft, Buddy gave me a heads up that the Mets would be in touch with a contract offer. She confided that while the team's top brass was not entirely sold on me, she'd overcome any remaining doubts and tipped the scale in my favor by telling the team's owner he would be enshrined in Cooperstown for breaking baseball's gender barrier if he green lit my signing, destined to be hailed as the "Branch Rickey for women in baseball."

I wasn't exactly a huge bonus baby, given a perfunctory $25,000 to sign a minor league deal when others with my high school stats might be getting millions if they wore a jockstrap rather than a sports bra under their uniforms. My parents were furious, insisting the positive press and merchandising opportunities alone were worth at least 10 times what I was offered, noting that video of my Mets tryout had gone viral and drawn 1.5 million views. But this was one offer I couldn't refuse. I didn't care about the money as long as I got a chance to play professional baseball. What if I turned down the Mets to go to college and didn't pitch well, or hurt my arm? Even worse, what if I pitched well and still no Major League team was interested? I might never get a chance like this again.

After going over all the possibilities, my parents said this was my decision to make—the biggest one of my life. But like you, Jackie, I was never one to play it safe or do anything the easy way, so I bet on myself and signed with my hometown favorites. But Dad did get the Mets to kick in a percentage of Spikes-related merchandise sales—an unprecedented partnership for an undrafted free agent out of high school.

19

The initial reaction to my signing was predictable, with most of the mainstream press and baseball purists deriding the move as a "woke" publicity stunt doomed to undermine the game's integrity. Yet before long many others weighed in via social media, blogs, and podcasts, sharing clips of my dominance in high school and impressive Mets tryout, expressing excitement about this historic opportunity and dismissing critics as shameless sexists. All I could say over and over to those questioning my bona fides was that baseball remains a meritocracy. If I proved myself by excelling in the minors, I'd keep moving up and hopefully earn a shot at the majors.

And that's exactly what I did, Jackie, making my way each season from A-ball in Brooklyn to AA in Binghamton, then AAA in Syracuse. I always struggled at first as I adjusted to a higher level of competition before once again locking in and baffling hitters, my knuckler improving with every year of coaching and practice. And even though I encountered the same blind skeptics and anti-feminists each step of the way, I also built a massive following of true believers and rabid fans cheering me in person and across all digital platforms.

Which is why I'm here today at Citi Field, about to change baseball and the world at large, just as you did back in 1947.

Hang on, Jackie....There's someone knocking on my door... It's my publicist....I've got to meet with my sponsors, then do yet another press conference. We'll pick this up later, Jackie... Thanks for listening!

Chapter 4: 3 p.m.

Dear Jackie,

It's amazing I have any time free to play baseball, what with all the events I must attend for the media, the team, my sponsors, and charity work. Sometimes I feel more like a corporation than a ballplayer! While I'm grateful for the attention and income, most days baseball becomes an afterthought!

The only thing crazier than getting paid to play baseball for a living is getting paid a whole lot more for doing absolutely nothing except being yourself. The minute I signed with the Mets, sponsors circled like sharks, eager for a piece of me. But I rejected nearly all of them, not wanting to shill for just anyone and wary of becoming famous for being famous before I achieved anything more than showing up. Which is why I absolutely refused to publish an autobiography while in my teens, nor would I allow the movie rights to my life story to be optioned. I first want to make sure there's a happy ending!

Companies looked to capitalize on my fame, offering to pay me handsomely to slap the name "Spikes" on sneakers, tracksuits, tights, leggings, tank tops, hoodies, and gym bags, as well as perfume, cosmetics, handbags, and backpacks. I passed on them all for the moment, not wanting to appear greedy or presumptuous about my baseball future.

It wasn't until I enjoyed sustained success on the playing field and reached Triple-A, one step from the majors, that I finally gave in and approved a few commercial endorsements—but only for high-profile sponsors with products close to my heart. Topping the list was a "Spikes" action figure, complete with a baseball held in an authentic knuckler grip! A close second was seeing my face on a cereal box, with illustrations of how to throw my patented knuckleball on the back. Being added as a real-life player to baseball video games I'd played while growing up was way cool, as was having my own signature pitcher's mitt (blue for the Mets, not pink)! I also green-lit an illustrated children's book to show the next generation of empowered girls how they might follow my lead.

I must admit I was a bit star struck with the dozens of celebrities jumping on my bandwagon. Only a few of these surreal encounters mattered to me long term because the individuals involved didn't need to be seen with me to validate their status, and because they seemed genuinely interested in helping me succeed.

That short list included President Donald Cumberland, who invited me to the White House, where I slept in the Lincoln Bedroom! I know you spoke with President Eisenhower in the Oval Office back in 1957, Jackie, and came away frustrated by his cautious approach to civil rights, but I think you would love

President Cumberland. He's a serious baseball fan who had a decent college career as a catcher—which makes sense because that's the thinking man's position, and because catchers control the game just like Presidents do.

Since he keeps a batting cage in the White House basement, he insisted on taking a few dozen hacks against me! It was weird having a pair of armed Secret Service agents behind the cage flanking the most powerful person on Earth as he flailed away at my knuckler, but Cumberland was very gracious, laughing at his own futility. He winced and cried out when I bounced a pitch in the dirt that ricocheted off his knee—good lord, Jackie, I hit the President of the United States! That had to hurt, but he walked it off and dug right back in without complaint, managing to get good wood on a few of my final deliveries.

I also bonded with a group of accomplished women at a fashion magazine photo shoot, all eager to offer advice and take me under their wing. The cover story was to be headlined: "Spikes Randall Takes On Baseball's All-Boys Club," playing on my nickname by having me wear ridiculously high stiletto heels on which I could barely stand, while clad in a super short, chic, backless, sheer, silvery gown showing lots of leg and barely covering my butt. On the cover and inside spread, I was surrounded by a bevy of beautiful, talented females who had overcome obstacles to conquer their own fields, sporting similarly towering footwear and eye-catching designer outfits.

My fellow trailblazers included Yuja Wang (the Lady Gaga of classical music, who offered tips on becoming a fashion icon and launching my own clothing line), Misty Copeland (the first

Black principal dancer in American Ballet Theater, who advised me to create my own foundation providing scholarships and equipment for qualified girls attending baseball camps around the country—financed by my sponsors), and Sabrina Ionescu (the New York Liberty's superstar sharpshooter, who suggested I run clinics on how to throw a knuckleball, leveling the playing field by giving more girls a chance to compete with harder throwing boys).

But perhaps the most amazing encounter was with my all-time favorite pop singer, Taylor Swift, who reached out to say she was such a huge fan that she wrote a song about me, later inviting me onstage and singing it while we danced together at her concert in Madison Square Garden! Naturally, "Don't Mind Me and My Spikes" shot immediately to the top of the charts while prompting over a million Swifties to follow me on social media. Many of them started showing up to cheer wildly whenever I was scheduled to pitch, serenading me as our mutual pop idol's song blasted over the public address system while I took my warmups on the mound.

I realize this is all INSANE, Jackie! I'm just a baseball player, after all. But baseball today is a whole different world than what you dealt with, filled with "brand extensions" that turn an individual celebrity into an industry. Everything is riding on my success, and not just my fleeting fame or commercial sponsors. If I end up as a flash in the pan, that could slam the door in the face of all those girls counting on me to prove women belong here, just as you proved that for Blacks. I can't let them down!

It doesn't help that the press won't let me forget my precarious position. Every time I had a poor outing in the minors, all the doubters resurfaced. Had the league "figured me out"? Was my knuckler an illusion unlikely to fool professional hitters for long? Was it right for me to be dubbed, "The Female Jackie Robinson," when I wasn't Black? I had to keep reminding them I didn't call myself anything of the sort—that was just how President Cumberland introduced me in front of the cameras when greeting my arrival at the White House! And I came right back at them, wondering what difference it made that you and I aren't the same color? Aren't we all just part of the human race?

The celebrity reporters who knew nothing about baseball would always ask why I'm called "Spikes." I told a few of them it's because I was tough, mean, and downright dangerous, raising my spiked shoes to scare off or cut fielders who dared try to tag me out. But the regular sports media knew that as a pitcher I never hit or ran the bases, so I had to 'fess up and tell them the true story—that it was my mom who gave me that nickname when I first started playing Little League, complaining about how I kept scraping our wood floor by forgetting to take off my spikes after a game. "She'd wear them to bed if I let her," Mom would always say.

The worst part of doing interviews was the media's obsessive speculation about my love life—which, to be honest, is non-existent. Every time I went out on a date, there were just too many eyes and cameras on me. And the questions were so rude and ridiculous! Have I ever slept with a teammate? (Absolutely not!) Would I ever date a star from another sport? (Like who? Can you hook us up?) Was it true I turned down a TV reality show's offer of $5 million for a chance to meet "the man of my dreams" (it was), and did I say no because I was already committed to someone? I keep explaining I don't have time for romantic drama right now—but that doesn't stop them from suggesting I may be involved with every D-list celebrity who insists on taking a picture with me to give their career a boost, or from printing lies about those claiming to have been my lover in high school or the minor leagues, most of whom I'd never even met!

Then there's the inevitable query asked of all female athletes, with or without a boyfriend: Am I gay? (No! Not that there's anything wrong with that!) One obnoxious reporter had the nerve to demand proof that I'm not transgender, citing vague rumors to the contrary about treatments I'd undertaken at some clinic in Europe. I've never even left the country, let alone changed sexes!

At some point, I'd lose my patience with all the prurient probing and turn the tables by challenging the press to investigate more important topics, such as:

Why am I the only female player in the big leagues, and what took so long for a girl like me to get here?

Why isn't Major League Baseball doing more to attract and develop women in the sport?

Why isn't there at least one woman coaching first or third base in the majors, or any female umpires when the NBA and NFL have referees sporting ponytails? And why aren't more women calling play by play in the broadcast booth?

Why isn't there a professional women's baseball league modeled after the WNBA, to inspire more girls to play hardball in little league, high school, and college?

And why is there only one woman in the Hall of Fame—that being an owner from the Negro Leagues, ironically named Effa *Manley*? Oh, sure, the Hall has that exhibit on women in baseball that helped change my life. But unlike the overdue induction of Negro League stars, no player from the real life "League of the Their Own" has been similarly honored with a bronze plaque. That has to change!

I ended the press conference by saying that the most important achievement for me in making the majors is encouraging more and more young girls to play hardball if that's their dream. I'm proud to see how the flood of young girls enrolling in baseball programs has risen to a tidal wave since I'd signed.

Sorry, Jackie, but that's my parents at the door! I wouldn't be here without them.

Chapter 5: 4 p.m.

"You talking to Jackie again, Kristy?"

"Beats staring at these bare walls, Dad."

"Wow! It's pretty tight quarters in here!"

"It's where I changed as a ballgirl, Mom....At least it has a shower."

"I'll speak with the general manager about this after the game! The team's star attraction shouldn't be stuck in a broom closet!"

"I'm fine, Mom, I swear! Don't make a big fuss over this! Most of the guys already probably think of me as some kind of diva."

"We sure have come a long way, Kristy....It seems like just yesterday I got you your first mitt after we watched Mo'ne Davis pitch in the Little League World Series, and baseball is all you would think about!"

"I appreciate everything you've done for me, Dad! I know you probably would've preferred having a son, but I turned out pretty good, right?"

"Are you kidding? You've been a blessing for your mother and I since you were born. We're so proud of you!"

"Hey, Dad, remember there's no crying in baseball!"

"There will be tonight when I see you take that mound!"

"Seriously, Dad, I appreciate all the time you took away from your work to see my games and practice with me while I was a kid. And then you sold your insurance agency to manage my career and finances."

"That was a no-brainer, kiddo! Running Team Spikes is a full-time job I wouldn't trust to anyone else. I keep an eye on your agent, accountant, publicist, and social media coordinator so you can concentrate on baseball."

"You're not only my biggest fan, Dad. You're also my chief troubleshooter! Whatever obstacles stand in my way, you always figure out how to get past them. If you hadn't come up with the idea of turning me into a knuckleballer and found someone to teach me the pitch, I wouldn't be here."

"I didn't raise you by myself, you know."

"Mom, you're just as special to me as Dad, but in different ways. I got my athleticism and competitive drive from you—a Las Vegas showgirl who became the best personal trainer in Brooklyn!"

"Lucky for us I met your father at one of his insurance conventions or I'd probably still be working in Vegas!"

"You had me working out with you just about every day as soon as I could walk, whether at the gym or in the pool, running track or biking for miles at a time, all to build up my arms and legs equally."

"I handled you the same as any of my other clients, balancing strength with flexibility, combining weights with stretching."

"You're also a damned good cook!"

"I learned to cook because I wanted to make sure you ate right…"

"…while filling me up with vitamins and legal supplements to enhance my strength and stamina! You still won't let me eat junk food!"

"I also made sure you took your schoolwork seriously so that you'd have a good education to fall back on…"

"…because no matter how good I was at sports, you always reminded me that hardly any teenage athletes make it to the pros, and even fewer succeed even if they somehow get that far."

"And after spending my childhood in dance class and kid acts, I made sure you had a life outside of baseball. I miss our girl-days-out—the massages and facials at the spa…hair and makeup at the beauty parlor…although it broke my heart that because you were a pitcher, I couldn't do anything fancy with your nails."

"Dad and I could've watched sports all day if you'd have let us, but you insisted on taking me to the ballet, opera, and Broadway shows...sticking novels and history books in my hands at bedtime so I'd read about something besides baseball and Jackie Robinson."

"Edna Mae, we should go and let Kristy get ready for the game. The pitching coach is cooling his heels in the hallway waiting for us to scram!"

"We love you, Kristine! Kick some ass out there!"

"I love you, too, Mom! And Dad, try not to cry tooooo much when I take the mound. You know the TV cameras will be showing closeups of your reaction."

"We'll try not to embarrass you, superstar! Just don't forget to have fun while you're out there! Those big lugs will be like putty in your hands!"

Chapter 6: 5 p.m.

Dear Jackie,

My pre-game meeting didn't take long. Since I only throw a knuckler—rarely if ever attempted by anyone else—pitching coaches have no idea what advice to offer. Other pitchers study reams of data and analytic graphics, dissecting each opposing hitter's strengths and weaknesses, preferred pitches and locations, quirks and tendencies. But nobody's strength is hitting a knuckler; more likely it's everybody's weakness. Besides, I've never had a pitching coach who handled a knuckleballer before or have a clue about how to wield its magical powers. Mostly they talk about "staying within myself," whatever the hell that means. Who else would I stay within?

The only one I can depend on for an expert opinion is my personal catcher, Johnny LaFontaine, a real-life Crash Davis. Like Kevin Costner's gruff but savvy character in "Bull Durham," Johnny is a 34-year-old baseball vagabond who's played for eight organizations since flaming out as a first-round pick from Lincoln's arch rival, Lafayette.

Wherever I've pitched, from Little League to the majors, catchers run for the showers, not wanting any part of me, fearful of breaking a finger or looking foolish as they struggle to corral my knuckleball. Most would rather follow Bob Uecker's advice that the best way to catch a knuckler is to wait until it stops rolling and then pick the ball up! But Johnny didn't shy away.

Johnny showed up the day I was promoted to Double-A sporting an oversized mitt designed to snare knucklers, eagerly volunteering for this thankless, unenviable gig. The only complaint I ever heard from Johnny was that the stress of catching my knuckleball gave him streaks of premature gray in his wavy, jet-black hair. But that was a worthwhile sacrifice, because in Johnny's eyes being the only fool on the team—and perhaps the entire Mets organization—who wanted to catch my uncatchable pitch could be his ticket to finally make it up to The Show.

LaFontaine was indeed Johnny on the spot, studying the mysteries and anatomy of my knuckler like a baseball forensic scientist. He broke down my every movement, habit, and nuance both live and on video to the point where he could recognize problems in my grip and delivery before I noticed that anything had gone awry, while able to suggest corrections on the fly in warmups and even during games.

"Okay, Spikes!" he'd bark in the bullpen. "Let's see how badly you can screw with these batters' heads tonight with that crazy ass pitch of yours." After warming me up, we'd enter the game together, and as a result Johnny logged far more innings behind the plate than he ever would have otherwise. He told me more than once that if I hadn't come along, and he hadn't been desperate enough to catch me, he likely would've been released and seen his disappointing career come to an ignoble end. But as a key part of our dynamic duo, with any luck we'd make our major league debuts together. Which is exactly what we're doing today after both being called up from Triple-A to replace a pair of Mets relievers who went down with sore elbows.

That's not to say Johnny is undeserving. Quite the contrary! He's the proverbial Quadruple-A player—too good at calling a game, coaxing pitchers through tough stretches, and throwing out runners to be in Triple-A, but not a good enough hitter to make the majors, with a career minor league average below .200. I felt a lot more confident about my chances with Johnny behind the plate, and I'm grateful to the Mets for recognizing that and accommodating me. The last thing I wanted was for my historic debut to end with a passed ball that allows the game-winning run to score!

Once the pitching coach left, Johnny carefully filed my nails, which are critical to gripping the knuckler—a misnomer since knuckles have nothing to do with the pitch. Johnny had become quite an expert manicurist, taught the proper technique by my mother, who had handled my pitching hand exclusively until Johnny joined Team Spikes.

I couldn't wait to tell Johnny about running into Shohei Ohtani earlier in the day when the stadium was still empty. An all-star at the plate as well as on the mound, in broken English HE asked ME to show HIM how to throw my knuckleball! I must say his initial attempts generated some nasty movement! Is there anything the Great Ohtani can't do??? He laughed, bowed, and thanked me profusely, explaining that after two Tommy John surgeries, you never know when you might need a new pitch!

Did I forget to tell you we're playing the Dodgers, Jackie? Ain't that some wild karma?!? I know Brooklyn didn't treat you right at the end of your career, having the nerve to trade you to the Giants when your skills started to erode, pretty much forcing you into retirement. You certainly deserved better, Jackie, after everything you did for the team, the league, and the country.

That episode taught me no matter how good you were in your career, you'll get kicked to the curb the minute you falter. You're only as good as your last season...or game...or even your last inning or pitch. But at least the Dodgers gave you a chance, Jackie, and you made the most of it. I'm going to try to do the same, starting today.

Sorry, Jackie, but my bodyguards are here—a pair of former Secret Service agents recommended by President Cumberland himself! Just like you, I've had a bunch of death threats the police and FBI insist on taking seriously. Can you imagine people getting that crazy about a girl playing baseball?!? Anyway, it's time to head out to the bullpen. The game will be starting soon. Wish me luck!

Chapter 7: 8:30 p.m.

Dear Jackie,

Things were going so well. Sure, it was a circus atmosphere filled with way too much hoopla, from President Cumberland throwing out the first pitch to Taylor Swift singing the National Anthem! But it gave me chills to receive a standing ovation as I walked with Johnny up the first base line to the bullpen just before game time, the outpouring of support from devoted fans drowning out the few obnoxious catcalls from haters.

In the minors I was a starter, with a set routine to pitch every fifth day, but for now the team thinks I'd be better off as a reliever, giving the hitters less opportunity to adjust to my knuckler the second or third time through the lineup. Dad suspects it's more likely the front office figured they could draw more fans if I were able to come out of the bullpen on any given night. But whatever their reasoning, it was unnerving not knowing when I would pitch. I couldn't sit still in the bullpen. My legs kept fidgeting and I bit my nails down to the skin on my non-throwing hand as the game dragged on, dying to get this over with already.

We jumped out to a 5-0 lead, but when our starter faltered in the fifth and gave up back-to-back solo homers, the call came for me to warm up. I could hear the crowd buzzing with anticipation as the jumbotron above the scoreboard showed me climbing atop the bullpen mound, beginning to throw. They started chanting, "SPIKES! SPIKES!! SPIKES!!! SPIKES!!!!" while the Mets were still hitting!

Good lord, Jackie! This is really happening!!!

And then it happened, Jackie....The worst thing that could happen to a knuckleballer.

I broke a nail.

It's an occupational hazard, but the timing couldn't be worse.

Without a solid nail on my middle finger to dig into the surface of the ball, I can't grip it properly. If I can't grip it properly, the knuckler spins rather than flatlines out of my hand. If it spins, the ball's trajectory won't be influenced by changes in airflow caused by differences between the stitching and the smooth surfaces surrounding them. Without the resulting asymmetric drag, the knuckler won't flutter all over the place on its way to the plate like a drunken bird. And rather than leave the batter weak-kneed and helpless, a spinning knuckler will be like serving the ball up on a tee, inviting the hitter to crush it to only God knows where.

Someone's at the door, Jackie....

37

"Johnny? Oh, thank God! Mom, it's you!"

"Johnny called me after you bolted out of the pen, so I ran back here to check the damage! He's right behind me."

"Who the hell were you just talking to, Spikes?"

"My mother, of course!"

"No! Before then. You were already talking with someone when she opened the door."

"I was talking to myself."

"She was dictating messages to Jackie Robinson again! Been babbling away like this to him about her hopes and frustrations ever since she was a little girl. She became obsessed with him after her dad took her to his museum, convinced they're kindred spirits. She's got hours of recordings on her phone. She should turn them into a book someday."

"Does Jackie ever answer you back, Spikes?"

"Leave her be, Johnny. It's weirder than keeping a diary but cheaper than seeing a shrink."

"How bad is it, Mom?"

"It doesn't look good, Kristy. The nail is halfway split right down the middle. The whole thing could give way and tear off if you don't give it time to heal."

"Mom, please!!! I have to pitch tonight! How could I possibly chicken out now?!? The President of the United States landed his chopper in the outfield to make the game! There's press here from all over the world! The stands are packed and millions more are watching on TV or live streaming! Good lord, Taylor Swift is in the house!!!"

"Everyone may just have to wait a little longer to see you, Kristy. You must be at your best to beat major leaguers."

"But Mom! Think of the shame...the humiliation! What will people say if the first woman to make the majors had to blow off her debut because of a broken fingernail?!?"

"Pitchers miss games all the time because of a blister. This is no different."

"Mom, this is TOTALLY different! The only worse excuse would be blaming it on my period!!!"

"This is all my fault, Edna Mae! I knew I should've applied another coat of polish after filing her nails."

"Don't blame yourself, Johnny. I've been throwing too much lately for the TV cameras and publicity shots."

"Johnny may have a point, Kristy. Another coat might fortify it, at least for tonight...but not with your regular nail polish."

"You thinking what I'm thinking, Mom?"

"I keep a tube in my bag, just in case...but it's pretty old."

"Just do it, Mom! Desperate times call for desperate measures."

"What the hell is that, Edna Mae? Jeez! You're not actually going to put super glue on your kid's fingernail?"

"I've done it a couple of times before, Johnny, but not since she signed to go pro. It's a lot stronger than regular beauty parlor glue, which is fine for tea party emergencies, but won't hold up under the stress she'd put on the nail to grip her knuckler."

"Is this even legal?"

"I have no idea, Johnny. But I don't have a choice if I want to get back out there tonight."

"Ain't that stuff dangerous to your health?"

"I doubt it's doctor recommended, Johnny."

"Are you sure it won't kill you?"

"Maybe...but it won't kill me tonight, while the fans and the press might form a lynch mob if I bail out now."

"Just make sure not to get any of that stuff on the ball! The last thing we need is for you to get tossed from the game and suspended for using a foreign substance!"

"It dries super-fast and super-hard, Johnny! No one will even know it's there except us."

"It's done, Kristy! Blow on it, and let's hope for the best."

"What if the glue doesn't hold, Edna Mae?"

"It'll just have to, Johnny."

"But what if it doesn't? We gotta have a Plan B, Spikes."

"Like what? I don't have time to boost my velocity to the high-90s with steroids!"

"Well, you could finally test drive that split-finger pitch we've been playing with."

"Seriously? We've only tried it in the bullpen."

"No time like the present... Weren't you the one talking about desperate times? The splitter is called the 'pitch of last resort' for a reason."

"Kristy, you're not talking about throwing a spitball, are you?"

"It's a *splitter*, Mom, not a *spitter*."

"Teams discourage splitters because they keep blowing out pitcher's elbows, Edna Mae."

"Only if you rely on it most of the time, Johnny....But I suppose it couldn't hurt to mix it in tonight. We may have no other choice."

"How does the splitter work, Kristy?"

"It's a fastball delivery, Mom, thrown with the same arm speed.... Yet if I spread my first two fingers wide around the seams, it may look like a fastball coming towards the hitter, but if thrown correctly the bottom drops out and it goes straight down before it reaches the plate. Fools batters almost every time."

"Ohtani uses it as his put-away pitch, Edna Mae."

"And has two Tommy John surgeries to show for it, Johnny!"

"Then we won't make a habit of it, Mom.... All right, Johnny. We'll keep the splitter as Plan B....But only as a last resort!"

"Gotcha, Spikes.... I just texted the manager and pitching coach that you're good to go.... Looks like they're going to hold you back until the ninth inning."

"They want me to close the game?!?"

"At the moment, we're still up a run. They figure since you're a knuckleballer trained as a starter, you could pitch until you drop if the Dodgers tie it up and we go extra innings."

"But this nail likely won't last more than a few batters, Johnny, let alone a few innings!"

"Then you'll just have to finish them off one, two, three! Let's go!!!

Jackie, would you please pray for me? Here goes nothing!

Chapter 8: 10:30 p.m.

Dear Jackie,

What a night! I'm drenched, both in sweat and champagne! Soaked right through my uniform! But I don't mind. I'm just so happy it's over!!!

The positive energy emanating from the crowd was palpable when I stepped out of the bullpen in the top of the ninth inning, proud to be wearing your number 42 like all the other players honoring you on Jackie Robinson Day. Jogging across the rightfield grass, I was greeted by a groundswell of cheers as my Taylor Swift anthem blared throughout the stadium. Not since Timmy Trumpet heralded the entrance of Mets closer Edwin Diaz had there been such an uproar for a relief pitcher.

Yet the pandemonium reached a whole other level when I climbed atop the mound, with the public address announcer bellowing above the din: "Now pitching for your New York Mets, making her Major League debut, the First Lady of Baseball, SPIKES RANDALL!!!"

Johnny LaFontaine gently draped his long, hairy arm around my shoulders to settle me down, grinning wide as the umpire handed me the ball. "Ain't this a hoot?" he shouted in my ear. "Let's show these guys what all the fuss is about!"

The Citi Field mound should've been familiar to me after all the time I'd spent throwing BP as a ballgirl, Jackie, yet it felt as high as a mountain tonight. No one paid any attention to a batting practice pitcher in a near empty stadium. But now the eyes of millions were focused on every move I made.

I didn't feel anything amiss with my split nail as I warmed up. I didn't really feel anything at all—my bloodstream flooded with adrenaline, overwhelmed to have finally arrived at my destination, willing my mind to focus on the trio of batters waiting to face me—a modern Murderers Row!

The Baseball Gods certainly didn't make it easy for me, Jackie, facing the top-three Dodgers in the lineup, each one sure to be elected to the Hall of Fame five years after laying down their bats for good. We were only up 5-4, so I couldn't afford any mistakes, not with the potential tying run coming to the plate and the winning runs on deck.

The leadoff hitter was Mookie Betts, on the small side at five feet, nine inches, but all muscle at 180 pounds and packing quite a punch. He hits wherever the ball is pitched—you can neither tie him up inside nor entice him to chase away, overpower or jam him. He sprays singles and doubles all over the outfield and runs like the wind, yet also has tremendous power, hammering over 400 homers. He has an eagle eye and uncanny command

45

of the strike zone, which means he won't swing if my knuckler strays too far from the plate.

Mookie is also a super-friendly guy who exudes a little kid's love for the game. Smiling brightly as he dug his right foot into the batter's box, he winked to let me know he was ready. "Let's make some history, as I hit the first homer off a girl!"

Flashes were going off like mad as everyone tried to capture my first pitch on their phones. I had barely warmed up in the pen, fearful of my nail giving way and not wanting to waste a single pitch. But here on the real mound I dug the tips of my index and middle fingers just above the seams as hard as I could, took a deep breath, wound up, and tossed one of my best knucklers.

It's amazing how so much effort goes into throwing a pitch that takes so long to reach the plate. Mookie's eyes narrowed as he cocked his bat, only to hesitate and freeze as he watched my knuckler break perfectly for strike one!

"Damn, girlie!" Mookie grinned, shaking his head, before turning to Johnny. "I'd like to see her try to get that son-of-a-pitch past me again!"

Mookie planted his right foot a little deeper in the batter's box and crouched down a bit to buy some extra milliseconds and gain more leverage for his swing. He unleashed a mighty uppercut at my next knuckler, which darted away from his bat as if it had eyes, landing unharmed in Johnny's giant mitt for strike two.

Mookie stopped smiling. He called for his one timeout and

stepped away, nodding as if he had figured me out, confident he would nail me next time. He stepped back in, moving up in the box, hoping to hit the knuckler a split second earlier, before it made its final break. He choked up on the handle for better bat control and accelerated speed, altering his swing to swat at the pitch. Yet Mookie just barely managed to make contact, tapping the ball right back to me on one lazy bounce. I snagged it in my mitt as I stumbled off the mound, able to recover just in time to fire the ball to first base for out number one!

"Gonna getcha next time, Spikes!" Mookie promised, jogging past me on his way back to the third base dugout. Yet rather than making me more confident, getting that first out left me in a daze, like a boxer stung by a sudden punch in the face. Johnny rose from his crouch and called out to me, but I couldn't hear a word he said over the deafening crowd noise. I waved him away before he could call for time and gathered myself on the rubber, checking my nail quickly while regaining my grip, only to look up and see the umpire step from behind the plate and wave his arms for a pitch clock violation! I had taken too long between hitters, with ball one allotted to the new batter.

And what a batter he was! Freddie Freeman was long and lean, curling his bat behind his left shoulder, ready to twist and explode at me like a snake about to strike. Although Freddie was pushing 40, he was as dangerous as ever. He looked huge compared to Mookie at the plate, at 6 feet, five inches and 220 pounds. He reminded me of the Tarzan character I read about as a kid, sinewy yet graceful. He was all business—no smiles, just a steady glare peeking out from under the bill of his Dodger blue batting helmet. He was approaching the rarified 500 home

47

run plateau, yet was no free swinger, with an average topping .300 and often much higher each season. Freddie is another aggressive hitter but doesn't chase balls out of the strike zone.

My first two deliveries were flat, but luckily bounced well in front of the plate before Freddie could make mincemeat out of them, bringing the count to 3-0. I didn't want to walk the tying run, putting the potential go-ahead run a homer away at the plate, so I threw just a little harder next time, which resulted in a little less break, figuring Freddie would take a pitch hoping to get on base. But he had other ideas, uncoiling with all his might, catching the underside of the ball as it darted away from him.

Freddie slammed his bat to the turf and ran to first base as the ball soared above home plate. Johnny tossed away his mask and stared into the heavens, patiently waiting for the pop fly to return to Earth. I hurried to his side as a backup, exhaling only after the ball landed safely in his oversized glove, barely in fair territory, for the second out.

It wasn't until I patted Johnny on the backside, leaving a small red stain on his butt, that I realized my nail was splitting again. I clenched my left hand in a fist, cursing to myself as Johnny called time and walked me back to the mound, his huge arm once again draped around my slim shoulders, asking how bad the damage was. I was beside myself, feeling tears of anger welling up—yet determined not to cry, knowing full well that TV cameras were zoomed in for a closeup of my face.

"I'm fine!" I insisted, speaking into my glove so no one could read my lips. When Johnny argued with me about getting the trainer out for a look, I snapped at him to get back behind the plate. By the time we were all in place, the bleeding had stopped but the skin beneath the damaged nail was a deep purple. Just great! As if it wouldn't be tough enough pitching to the game's greatest all-around player!

Shohei Ohtani stood patiently outside the batter's box, sporting his usual boyish grin. Even now, in his mid-30s, baseball's Japanese unicorn was still like an overgrown kid playing a children's game. Nothing seemed to faze him—certainly not hitting against a girl. He bowed slightly to me as our eyes met, holding up his right hand briefly to demonstrate the knuckleball grip I'd taught him before the game.

I had to smile despite the circumstances, which served to relax me. Just bear down but don't forget to have fun—that's what Dad told me before every game. Not since Ohtani had struck out his Angels teammate, Mike Trout, to close out Japan's victory over Team USA in the 2023 World Baseball Classic, had there been such a storybook confrontation.

Ohtani is another giant with uncanny bat speed and preternatural plate coverage. Pitch him inside and he'll pull the ball down the rightfield line into the second deck. Pitch him down the middle and he'll golf towering homers to deep centerfield. Pitch him away and he'll inside-out his swing to drive the ball to the opposite field without sacrificing any of his power. Like most lefty hitters, he preferred pitches down in the zone so he could just drop his bat head and launch balls into the stratosphere, but that didn't mean you could tie him up with high pitches. It's a wonder anyone ever got him out!

49

I gripped the ball as best I could with the tip of my index finger, while barely touching it with my middle fingernail, which by now was hanging on by a thread. I fully expected to release a batting practice pitch that Ohtani would crush onto the Shea Bridge over the right-centerfield fence.

But something weird happened that I never would've predicted. My velocity dropped to around 60 miles per hour from my usual 65-70, which normally would be a death knell. But instead, the knuckler behaved even more erratically than usual, darting sideways like a sweeper rather than zigzagging down towards the ground as usual. Ohtani lifted his front right leg to time the pitch, but it was no use. He couldn't pull the trigger as the knuckler snuck across the plate for strike one.

I shrugged at Johnny, who returned the gesture—we both knew from experience that my knuckler often had a mind of its own. Ohtani took a deep breath and his eyes narrowed, boosting his concentration as he swung at the next delivery, which veered horizontally even more sharply and well beyond Shohei's long reach for strike two.

Unfortunately, that unhittable pitch also took what was left of my damaged nail with it, prompting Johnny to call time and rush to the mound.

"We gotta get you outta here now!" Johnny insisted.

"I'm not quitting in the middle of an at-bat, a strike away from winning the damned game," I shouted back through my mitt.

"You can't throw your knuckler without a freakin' nail!" Johnny hissed through his mask, his face red and streaked with sweat.

"Then we'll go with Plan B," I said, as the umpire jogged to the mound to break us up. "I'll roll the dice with the splitter. I'll throw it as hard as I can and hope for the best."

Johnny shrugged and moved reflexively to slap my behind, but caught himself just short of contact, like a batter checking his swing to avoid a called strike.

"If you don't get this batter, we're done. Got it?"

He didn't wait for me to argue, turning to hurry back to his position just before the umpire reached the mound. I gripped the ball inside my glove, spreading my index and middle fingers so wide around the seams that it hurt, but not nearly as much as it would if I tried another knuckler without a fingernail. Where the ball would go—or end up going when Ohtani was done with it—I couldn't imagine. We'd experimented with the splitter with some success, but never against live batters.

No one at Citi Field was sitting at this point—not in the stands, the press box, or on either bench. Ohtani called time and stepped out, but I remained glued to the rubber, maintaining my unfamiliar grip, staring intently between Johnny's legs as he pumped his fist in encouragement. If Ohtani knew anything was wrong with me, he certainly didn't show it. The boyish grin was replaced by a poker face. He was all business and locked in, but so was I.

51

I closed my eyes briefly and took a deep breath, wound up, and fired away with a loud grunt, like a tennis player delivering a monster overhand serve. With all the adrenaline coursing through me, I somehow ramped up to 75 on the radar gun — the hardest I'd ever thrown a pitch, but still batting practice speed for Major League hitters. Ohtani's eyes went wide with recognition at the sudden rise in velocity and straightened trajectory, no doubt giddy to be spared the tantalizing flutter of my knuckler.

The splitter dove at the last minute just as it was designed to do. Shohei instinctively adjusted and golfed at the pitch, but he would've needed a shovel rather than a driver to make contact as it hit the dirt. Johnny somehow scooped up the loose ball as it skidded across the plate, bobbling it precariously for a moment like a live hand grenade. He hugged it up against his chest with both hands as if his life depended on it.

STRIKE THREE!

GAME OVER!!!

Johnny and the rest of the Mets stormed the mound as if we'd just won the World Series! I wouldn't have survived being buried beneath a pileup of these mammoth men, but Johnny got there first, lifting me onto his shoulders and parading me around the infield. Fireworks exploded above the Citi Field scoreboard, showing closeups of the bedlam on the field. The more than 42,000 fans on hand kept chanting, "SPIKES! SPIKES!! SPIKES!!! SPIKES!!!! SPIKES!!!!!" Even the defeated Dodgers stuck around, taking in the moment. After Johnny put me down, Shohei Ohtani made his way to my side, gave me a high five, and posed for some pictures—the epitome of class and good sportsmanship.

I made my way to the stands by our dugout, where Mom and Dad were waiting, hugging me so tight I almost couldn't breathe. Mom checked my bloodied finger, but then we both just laughed and jumped up and down with glee and relief. I was hurried over to a secure spot beneath the dugout roof, where President Cumberland congratulated me and held up my right arm like a victorious boxer. Someone from the Hall of Fame asked for my cap and spikes to display in Cooperstown, but I refused to surrender the ball Johnny caught to end the game, which was likely worth millions. Taylor Swift was handed a mike in her luxury box behind home plate and led the crowd in a triumphant rendition of my anthem.

The commissioner of baseball led me back onto the field by the mound to present a plaque commemorating the shattering of the national pastime's gender barrier, but I can't recall a word he said. I was simply dumbfounded. When it was time for me to address the delirious crowd, everyone went suddenly silent so as not to miss a word. Tears flowed down my cheeks, for which I felt no shame. My mom was trying to hold it together, but my dad was bawling his eyes out. He wasn't alone, as there weren't many dry eyes at the ballpark.

"I guess there is crying in baseball after all," I said, my voice choked with emotion, sending the fans into another frenzy, giving me time to pull myself together and go on with my speech.

"Just as the WNBA's Sabrina Ionescu said after facing Steph

Curry in a three-point showdown back in 2024, 'If you can shoot, you can shoot. It doesn't matter if you're a boy or girl.' It's the same with baseball. If you can pitch, you can pitch. So, I hope to see lots more of you girls in the stands today join me in this league before I'm through!"

Before I could utter any other words of wisdom or deliver more pithy quotes, Johnny came up behind me and stuffed a shaving cream pie in my face, while moments later Francisco Alvarez dumped a cooler of ice water over my head.

The on-field festivities finally over, I planned to return here to my solo space so I could clean up before meeting the press. But the team ambushed me, carrying me over their heads to the Mets locker room, where bottles upon bottles of champagne were uncorked, most of which were sprayed and poured on me! My eyes burned from the alcohol bath, but I didn't mind. I could've celebrated with my teammates all night, one of them at last.

The media was waiting impatiently, so my publicist pulled me from the party and took me straight to the press conference. I stood at the podium, dripping wet and shivering a bit until the hot TV lights took away the chill. I thanked my parents, coaches, and especially Johnny, congratulating him on his long overdue big-league debut. I thanked the fans for their support, as well as all those pioneering girls who came before me—including Mo'ne and Chelsea. And of course I took a moment to thank you again, Jackie, for being my inspiration and standing with me the whole way, if only in spirit.

I answered the usual assortment of lame questions about how I felt, as if a moment as special as this could be reduced to mere words. I kept repeating that all I ever hoped for was to be judged by what I can do, rather than what I am. All I ever wanted, I insisted, is to be just one of the boys.

Of course, Jackie, I realize that's a pipe dream. Like you, I'll always stand out, no matter what I achieve, for better or worse. But as long as I get to play, I couldn't care less.

Good lord, Jackie! I'm checking my phone, and an image of me has already gone viral. There's a shot showing me at the podium, soaked to the skin, my uniform top clinging to every curve, and my boobs prominently outlined.

The meme is headlined, "Just one of the boys?"

I suppose some things will never change, Jackie. Boys will be boys. But at least baseball will never again be an all-boys club.

Afterword: My Journey With Spikes

Captain Ahab obsessed over his great white whale in "Moby Dick." King Arthur's knights risked life and limb to retrieve the Holy Grail. Don Quixote tilted at windmills, ready to "march into hell for a heavenly cause." My own decades-long quest has been far more modest yet seemed equally hopeless—to write a piece of fiction about Spikes Randall, the first woman to play Major League Baseball. But with this, my latest version, I believe I've finally captured my white whale, secured the elusive grail, and beaten those damned windmills once and for all!

Why was I so determined to write this story in the first place, and felt compelled to keep coming back to rewrite it again and again over the years?

I've always been a big fan of women in sports, from Mary Lou Retton to Simone Biles in gymnastics, Gabriela Sabatini to Coco Gauff in tennis, and most recently Sabrina Ionescu to Caitlin Clark in basketball, while rooting for dozens of other heroines competing on the playing field and the courts. I imagine this comes from being raised by an athletic, single mom who had been a dancer and acrobat in vaudeville, combined with the sex appeal of childhood crushes on tomboys with whom I played punchball and touch football. So, it's no wonder the notion of females playing my favorite sport of baseball has long been a fascination of mine.

I've followed the slow but steady rise of women in America's national pastime with great interest. I showed up early at Shea Stadium in 1995 to see the Colorado Silver Bullets, a barnstorming team of professional women, play a group of Mets old timers. I was riveted to the TV in 2014 watching 13-year-old Mo'ne Davis become the first girl to pitch a shutout in the Little League World Series. I devoured the biography and saw an Off-Broadway play about Toni Stone, who played second base during the Negro League's final seasons. And one of my favorite movies of all time is "A League Of Their Own," based on the true story of a female professional hardball league formed during WWII. (Geena Davis can play for my team anytime!)

Meanwhile, I've kept tabs on the exploits of various women playing with men in independent leagues unaffiliated with the majors, such as Ila Borders (the first woman to win a college baseball game before going pro) and Kelsie Whitmore (who has played for three pro teams in Sonoma, Staten Island, and Oakland). There have also been a bunch of female coaches and executives of late for Major League teams—including Rachel Balkovec (who managed a low level Yankees' minor league affiliate) and Kim Ng (the first female general manager, serving from 2021 through 2023 with the Florida Marlins).

Yet as I write today, 77 years after Jackie Robinson finally broke Major League Baseball's shameful color barrier, the sport remains devoid of female players, with no obvious candidate to follow in Jackie's groundbreaking footsteps. There hasn't even been a woman umpire yet, long after both the National Basketball Association and National Football League deployed female referees. Pam Postema, author of "You've Got To Have Balls To Make It In This League," almost made it, becoming the first woman to umpire a spring training game in 1988, but never took the field in a Major League game that counted. Hopefully Jen Pawol, just a step away from the Majors in AAA ball, will have better luck six years after I watched her umpiring home plate, her ponytail bobbing behind her, during a High-A Brooklyn Cyclones game.

Of course, this time it's not just sexism holding women back— it's also the lack of opportunity for girls and young women to get the training and experience needed to prepare them for a shot at the Major Leagues. When Jackie Robinson came to the Dodgers, he and the parade of Black players following him had honed their skills in their own segregated yet high level professional league. Women don't have that option. Meanwhile, many girls are still often steered into softball as kids.

Not that there's anything wrong with playing softball, which certainly isn't "soft" given how hard women throw under-handed. But hardball is a different game requiring a unique skill set, which far too few females have a chance to develop. That's changing, with groups such as Baseball For All promoting gender equity for girls by providing opportunities to play and coach hardball. And there is also a Women's World Cup baseball tournament to which players may aspire.

Imagine A World With Women In The Major Leagues

For the moment, however, the notion of a woman playing Major League Baseball alongside men remains a fantasy, one that's not often envisioned even in fictional books, TV shows, or movies. Long ago I decided to challenge that lack of imagination by writing "Spikes," which started out ambitiously as a novel, but stalled because the narrative kept veering off into soap opera territory, with love affairs and petty jealousies intruding on the baseball action.

Since I couldn't come up with enough compelling baseball material to carry an entire novel, I decided instead to recast "Spikes" as a short story, focusing on the main character's dramatic debut. But even then, the action became bogged down with too many extraneous and even ridiculous plot twists, such as having an evil (female) owner who trumped up death threats to generate publicity and boost attendance, only to have an actual assassination attempt take place at the ballpark.

Another major obstacle was that I shied away from using real teams and current players. I placed Spikes on a fictional baseball team, the Brooklyn Eagles, on the grounds of Coney Island's old Steeplechase amusement park, where the Cyclones play as a Mets' affiliate. As a result, the story lacked authenticity. It felt fake.

To make matters worse, I began to have doubts about my ability to pull this story off. After all, while I was a successful business journalist and financial services researcher for 43 years, writing mostly about the insurance industry and risk management, I

59

remained an amateur with fiction. I authored two novels in the early 1980s (one of which was shopped around by a professional agent), but neither of them sold.

All I knew for sure was that while truth may indeed be stranger than fiction (as epitomized by the expression, "You can't make this stuff up"), truth is easier to write. Journalists and researchers gather verifiable facts, analyze hard data, and interview real people to write their reports. With fiction, writers must create believable characters and plausible scenarios out of whole cloth.

I kept coming back to "Spikes" every few years but set it aside for good (or so I thought) in 2016, after Fox announced it was producing a TV drama called "Pitch," about (you guessed it) the first woman to play in the majors. I was pretty bitter about that, but actually liked the show, only to see it canceled after one season for some of the same reasons why my own version failed to take off.

Like my story, "Pitch" ended up being more of a soap opera since there wasn't enough baseball narrative to support a weekly series. "Pitch" also posed an authenticity problem, since neither of our heroines were likely to throw hard enough to believably contain Major League hitters—especially these days, when 100 miles-per-hour pitches are becoming the norm.

The Turning Point For 'Spikes'

Fast forward to my retirement in June 2023. Having nothing but time on my hands, I decided to give "Spikes" one more shot. I started from scratch, not even looking at prior versions, determined to rethink my entire approach and reinvent the story. For six months I pondered what I had done right and wrong during my initial attempts, coming up with solutions in one epiphany after another.

First, to make the story plausible, Spikes needed a legitimate "out" pitch. Inspired by the success of Cy Young Award winner R.A. Dickey of the Mets, I had her throw a knuckleball! Not only didn't a pitcher have to throw very hard (usually around 70-miles-per-hour), but so few threw knucklers that it consistently fooled most batters. The clincher came during my bucket list pilgrimage to Cooperstown, at the Baseball Hall of Fame's "Diamond Dreams" exhibit about the contribution of women to the game. There were pictures of Chelsea Baker, "The Knuckleball Princess," who tossed two perfect games as a 12-year-old Little Leaguer in 2010. A web search unearthed a video of Baker as a high school pitcher making Major League batters look foolish throwing batting practice to the Tampa Bay Rays in 2014.

Second, to make the story feel more authentic, I decided to use real teams and actual players. My research found that doing so shouldn't trigger any legal problems if the work is clearly marked as fiction, and as long as trademarked logos aren't used, false commercial endorsements aren't claimed or implied, and the individuals or organizations cited aren't unfairly mischaracterized, or falsely or maliciously presented in a negative light. (Quite the contrary! In my story, the Mets' owner is hailed as "The Branch Rickey for women in baseball," likely to be enshrined in Cooperstown.)

Third, who would tell the story? While I'd keep it relatively short to avoid falling into the inevitable soap opera trap (ending up as a novelette at around 13,500 words), I'd struggled over the years determining the point of view. In some versions, I had Spikes tell her own story, but wondered whether a male author should try to "speak" in the first person through a 20-year-old woman (an even trickier question in these hypersensitive times). So, I tried having her catcher narrate as he guides Spikes through her travails, but that made it his story rather than hers. In a third approach, I stayed in my comfort zone as a journalist, "reporting" the story as a series of articles and opinion columns filed by a sportswriter who was skeptical at first before becoming a wholehearted supporter. But that felt way too distant and detached from the woman making history, since he wasn't even in the arena with her.

After hitting those dead ends, I returned to writing a first-person narrative. Men write female characters all the time, and vice versa. Besides, I know Spikes better than anyone. I wanted her to tell her own story in her own voice so she could viscerally communicate to readers what she was seeing, experiencing, and feeling every step of the way.

There was just one more hurdle to overcome. How would Spikes tell her story?

Jackie Robinson To The Rescue!

Willie Mays is my favorite player of all time, but Jackie Robinson is my ultimate baseball hero. I never saw Jackie play outside of clips and one complete World Series game against the Yankees recorded for the ages, since he finished his relatively short yet historically impactful career 18 months before I was born. But I've always been fascinated with Jackie and filled with admiration for the courageous way he broke the color barrier in 1947, changing America in the process. I've read just about every book about him and gave my coveted 2013 "Sammy Award" for Best Picture to "42," the outstanding biopic starring the late, great Chad Boseman, who brought Jackie to life portraying the obstacles he faced on and off the field.

I had already decided that Jackie would be a hero to Spikes as well, inspiring her to challenge sex-based stereotypes and shatter baseball's seemingly unbreakable gender barrier. Jackie would be an imaginary kindred spirit to Spikes as she tried to follow in his footsteps, while learning from his difficult journey how to succeed against all odds and prejudices. Still, I was at a loss as to how to make the connection between them tangible and significant to the story beyond mere hero worship.

The solution came to me while reading "Emily Of New Moon" by L.M. Montgomery, a tale darker than another series of stories she'd written about one of my favorite fictional characters, Anne of Green Gables. Emily, like Anne, was an orphan, placed in a home whose occupants at first didn't want, understand, or appreciate her. Unlike Anne, however, who never knew her birth parents, Emily would write long, moving letters to her deceased father to cope with her loneliness, vent her fears and frustrations, as well as share her dreams of a better life.

So, I thought, why not have Spikes narrate the events of her groundbreaking Major League debut, along with highlights of how she'd finally reached that incredible moment, by dictating a series of letters to Jackie on her mobile phone before, during, and after her first game? She'd do so partly because she's nervous and is killing time sitting alone in her private locker room, but also to express her gratitude for the inspiration and example Jackie provided, which had given her hope and motivation to keep going against the discrimination and resistance they both had faced. Such an epistolary style would create a platform for Spikes to share her tale and triumph with her spirit guide.

I solidified the connection by sprinkling in other references to Jackie, making him a key character throughout the story. The mentions were organic, flowing naturally, almost as if Jackie is somehow looking out for her while creating a supernatural "Field Of Dreams" vibe. The clincher was adding a subhead to the title, "Spikes: The First Lady of Baseball, *As Told To Jackie Robinson*"—which I thought would grab the attention and pique the curiosity of potential publishers and readers alike.

I went to work and rewrote the story over four short weeks during March 2024. I've made multiple revisions since to sharpen the narrative, but am extremely satisfied with the result. No piece of writing is perfect, and "Spikes," I'm sure, is no exception. But at last I've produced a version that makes me happy, allowing me to check this huge box off my bucket list. I hope you enjoy reading it as much as I've enjoyed writing it.

One day I hope to see a real-life Spikes Randall take the field in a Major League game. A big step in that direction would be the launch of a professional hardball league for women, duplicating the outstanding success enjoyed by the Women's

National Basketball Association. The WNBA has given little girls, high school teens, and college women a legitimate pro league to shoot for, one where they can make a decent living and play the game they love at the highest level for large, enthusiastic crowds and millions more on TV.

How wonderful it would be to see a similar women's professional baseball league reconstituted, not only so girls would have a "league of their own" to aspire to, but also perhaps serving as a springboard preparing a new generation of women to play alongside men in the Major Leagues!

Let's hear it for "The Girls Of Summer"!

About the Author

Sam Friedman, a lifelong baseball fan, spent his 44-year professional career as a financial journalist and researcher, primarily as Editor in Chief at National Underwriter, and later as Insurance Research Leader at Deloitte. In retirement, he writes about sports, entertainment, and his life experiences in his blog, "Sam's View From The Press Box," while also revisiting the world of fiction, starting with this novelette, "Spikes."

You can connect with me on:

🌐 https://substack.com/@aviewfromthepressbox

🔗 https://www.linkedin.com/in/samoninsurance

Subscribe to my newsletter:

✉ https://substack.com/@aviewfromthepressbox

Made in the USA
Middletown, DE
06 September 2024

59880293R00042